Metaphorosis

May 2020

Beautifully made speculative fiction

Also from Metaphorosis

Metaphorosis Books

Reading 5X5 x2: Duets
Score – an SFF symphony
Reading 5X5: Readers' Edition
Reading 5X5: Writers' Edition

Metaphorosis Magazine

Metaphorosis: Best of 20xx
Metaphorosis 20xx: The Complete Stories
annual issues, from 2016

Monthly issues

Plant Based Press

Best Vegan Science Fiction & Fantasy
annual issues, from 2016

from B. Morris Allen:
Susurrus
Allenthology: Volume I
Tocsin: and other stories
Start with Stones: collected stories
Metaphorosis: a collection of stories

Metaphorosis

May 2020

edited by
B. Morris Allen

ISSN: 2573-136X (online)
ISBN: 978-1-64076-169-8 (e-book)
ISBN: 978-1-64076-170-4 (paperback)

Metaphorosis
a magazine of speculative fiction
from
Metaphorosis Publishing

Neskowin

May 2020

Figlia della Neve

Jonathan Louis Duckworth

The wife's eyes are closed, but there is no flutter of dream under her lids, and when her name escapes like a shy moth from the husband's tongue, she says, "Go on, I'm listening."

The husband begins his story.

The young man set out early one winter morning in search of the fabled Cold Lady. After hours of searching, he found her gliding through the silvered lindens and fell utterly in love. Her limbs were branches painted in winter's first frost.

Her long throat an egret considering the sun. Her skin was not what shimmered; it was the falling snow around her, crystalline flakes a swarm of prisms that made up her pearlescent aura. He was not the first to fall in love.

When she stopped to regard him, he gave her a white rose, which she breathed on, turning it silver with frost. This was custom—a man must present her with a white rose. She would breathe a hoarfrost upon the rose that would never thaw. If the man were to leave right there and then with the rose, and hang the rose over his bed, he would live a long life and never suffer nightmares. But few had ever left her. Instead they'd follow the lady again, until she stopped in her tracks once more to invite them to lead her to their homes. This is what the young man did: he followed her through the oaks and spruces and over a frozen river. Followed her even though he knew the innocent disaster she was. Followed her because love and disaster are voice and echo, echo and voice.

He had researched her assiduously. This Cold Lady wandered the Alps, had been sighted as far east as the Julian range in Yugoslavia, as far north as the

German border, and as far west as the slopes Mont Blanc. In Austria she was called *Das Schneemädchen*, while the French called her *La Dame Froide*. Here she was the Daughter of the Snow, *La Figlia della Neve*.

Despite what some claimed, her aura did not cause madness. The derangement already existed in the men who thought they could have her—who thought her life something that could belong to them. She was not alive. She was to life what light is to matter; what a metaphor is to reality.

"If she isn't alive, how does she exist?" the wife asks.

"As the stars do, burning lifelessly, tirelessly."

The young man had heard many versions of her origin. One story had it the lady of the snow was a priestess of a fertility Goddess's cult, punished for some forgotten transgression to forever wander the snow. Another claimed she was a victim of the Inquisition, which

9

supposedly accounted for her fear of fire. But her legend was older than the Inquisition. The old Celts who dwelled in the Alps before the Romans came shaped figures of her from clay, her tragic features crudely formed by hands that revered or pitied but never loved her, and love was what she needed, and, like any creature, deserved. It was as much compassion as mania that moved the young man to find her—to be the first warm, caring hand to ever hold hers.

Where she trod, even virgin snow hardened to ice. Many a man had broken a limb or worse following the slick of her path. The young man was careful with his steps as he followed. Birds compulsively built nests on the ground where she walked. The eggs never hatched, and foxes, cats, and martens that foraged them died as if poisoned. When winter ended and the spring thaw began, she'd retreat with the vestiges of winter into hollows carved into the mountains by ancient hands. In these lungs of the earth she'd slumber until the next snowfall.

The wife's voice is gossamer threading from her lips. "That sounds cozy."

The husband clears his throat and continues.

As was her custom, the lady invited her young suitor to show her to his home. They followed the old alpine trail down the slope, toward the village in the vale where smoke rose in gray whiskers from the chimneys. When they came to the village, to the sight of his cottage, she hesitated.

It was ever thus. Despite having followed a man willingly, the lady would always become anxious at seeing his home. Now was no different.

"It's too warm," she told the young man.

She had said this a thousand times.

This was what the young man knew: in all the stories, men were always too proud, too eager, too self-interested to heed her, and she was too desperate for a companion to refuse their urgings. Always the same. She would follow them inside, leaving a trail of frost over their threshold and up their staircase and into their bedrooms. They would make love, and then the men would hold her in their arms and fall asleep in the warmth of their beds. The men would wake feeling soaked, seeing the lady of the snow become translucent, then turning to water and seeping away into the sheets of the bed. Thereafter the men's hearts became hollow and frail. What is not living cannot die, but the men would not know this. Some would slit their throats on that very bed, desiring to mix their blood with her water. Others would walk outside, lie down, and wait for the falling snow to bury them. Some of these men were found and rescued with only minor frostbite. Others were discovered only after the snow melted. Meanwhile, the daughter of the snow had not died. She was reconstituted with the next snowfall, and the cycle continued. Her tears became a frosty rime around her eyes.

Knowing what he knew, the young man attempted something no one had before. He took her by the hand, led her into the house, and opened a window to let the cold air in.

"I want you to be comfortable," he told her.

She replied that it was still too warm for her. So he opened another window.

But it was still too warm. So he opened the door and left it open, and poured ashes over the smoldering fire in the grate. Finally, she told him she felt comfortable.

They went to the bed, and lay down together. The young man shivered, and the lady's body could offer him no warmth. She asked him if something was wrong.

He said nothing. He held her close, shivering, fighting to stay awake as the snow accumulated on the window sill and on the floor and invaded his bed. He fell asleep in her arms.

In the morning the young man awoke. He was not dead, and the girl had not melted. The window was closed. There was no sign of snow in the cottage. Beside him in the bed was a woman who looked like the lady. Just as beautiful and just as long-limbed, but ordinary in every way. Warm. Human.

"Good morning," he said.

"Good morning," she said back.

"Would you like some breakfast?" he asked her.

"I'd love some," she said, "it feels like forever since I've eaten."

And they lived a long, full, ordinary lifetime together.

When the husband finishes telling his story, he sees that his wife is beginning to stir, having fallen asleep briefly. The tiny flakes of snow slipping in through the half-opened bedroom window melt and radiate as vapor as they settle on her face. Last he checked a half hour ago, her temperature was the same as it has been these last few months: 102 degrees.

When she opens her eyes she looks at the white roses in the vase on her nightstand, and then smiles at her husband. "New ones?" she asks.

The husband nods. The flowers are from Chile, delivered on an airplane. The walls of their bedroom are plastered with crude crayon drawings from the children the wife used to teach when she was well. Happy scenes; sunny scenes, scribbled well-wishings.

"I'm sorry I didn't hear your whole story," she says.

"That's all right."

"I had a dream," she says. "I dreamed the fever had gone away."

He says nothing.

"Put your hand on my head. I want to feel a cold hand."

He takes one hand from its mitten and places it on her forehead. It is like touching an oven's window.

The doctors don't know what to call the wife's condition, which began in autumn as a seemingly ordinary fever that refused to diminish. All they know is that it is unlikely to be contagious, but likely to be fatal. One doctor termed it "hysterical cephalic hyperthermia." There is no cure. They've exhausted several experimental treatments with no results, while the fever boils her brain like an egg.

Cold air eases the wife's discomfort and helps her sleep, but this is a mere palliative. The husband has learned to live with the windows open, dressed in sweaters. It is late January now, and he fears the coming spring. There are air conditioners that can keep a room cold as winter, but they would have to be ordered from America and installed with great difficulty. The doctors keep trying to take her to a hospital, but neither the husband nor the wife want that. Last week, one of the doctors talked to the husband outside the house, and asked him if he was "making arrangements" yet.

"Did your story have a happy ending?" the wife asks.

"Yes," he lies. Fairy tales are happy only because they end before the end. Love is a stay of execution.

"That's good. When I'm better, and I go back to work, maybe you could visit my classroom and read your story for the children. I'm sure they'd like that."

He shakes his head. "I don't think it's good for children. Too sad."

"I thought you said it had a happy ending."

He says nothing.

"You should shave that beard. You don't look handsome with a big beard."

"It keeps me warm."

"Men don't look handsome with beards."

"I'll shave tomorrow."

"Fine," she said. "But will you bring me one of the cold apricots from the icebox?"

He doesn't want to leave her. For the moment, she's awake, but when he returns, who could know? He has a feeling as deep-set as the marrow of his bones that when his wife drifts off for good, he'll be taking a piss, whipping up some custard for her, on the telephone with one of the doctors, shaving, or bringing her apricots from the icebox.

But he stands up anyway.

"One more thing," the wife says, gesturing to the window.

The husband opens the window all the way. More snow blows in. When the husband returns with the apricot—hard and orange like a tiny frigid sun—the wife is asleep again. He wishes he could lie down beside her and crawl into her dreams. He wishes he could wake with her in a cold place where pools of frozen water have never known the touch of sunlight. But where she's gone, and where she's going, he cannot follow. And so the husband returns to his chair to watch the snow accreting on the window sill, wondering if his wife will remember him when she awakens again in the lightless lungs of the earth.

See Jonathan Louis Duckworth's story "Figlia della Neve" online at Metaphorosis.
If you liked it, leave a comment. Authors love that!

Remember to subscribe to our e-mail updates so you'll know when new stories are posted.

About the story

This story began from two sources: first, my reading of Angela Carter's fabulous collection *The Bloody Chamber and Other Stories*, and second, listening to a song from American power metal band Symphony X called "Lady of the Snow". The evidence of Carter's influence should be plain to anyone who's ever read her work. As for the song, it gave me the story's original title, "Lady of the Snow", when the story was still set in New England, rather than the Northern Italy locale of its current iteration.

I rewrote the story as "Figlia della Neve" because it fit well with a new story collection I've been putting together, a project called "Undying". Undying's central conceit is that all the stories are set in Europe (but not the British Isles) at some point between the mid 19th century and the 1970s. The collection's other central conceit is implied by the title: every story features some element of rebirth or resurrection, for good or for bad, and every story centers on the enduring, death-defying bonds of human attachment, again, for good or bad.

A question for the author

Q: Duckbilled platypus — result of divine distraction, or alternate universe crossover?

A: The platypus is the result of a beaver scientist and a duck mathematician attempting to divide by zero. There is a small organ called an oxylitic ganglion adjacent to the left sinus, unique among mammals, which allows the platypus to process mineral-heavy water and use it to produce pure DMT. By the time you have finished fact-checking this, I will have already made my escape.

About the author

Jonathan Louis Duckworth received his MFA in fiction from Florida International University. He is currently a PhD student at University of North Texas, studying poetry. He likes bending genres in his writing and has a deep passion for folklore and tall tales. His cat, Cheese, is very powerful and has an Instagram: @Misscheesevious

Regret's Relief

Travis Wade Beaty

I would have never gone to the Glyphs of Onyx if I hadn't fallen in love. I was in my final year at the University of Spell-Craft in Silver Forge. And as Silver Forge was the nearest port to the island of Onyx, and as the glyphs had been discovered only five years prior, students were always taking little holidays up there to see them. Most returned unimpressed. The Onyxian parliament itself had investigated the glyphs and not only had they concluded there was no magic to them, but also questioned whether they held any meaning whatsoever. Still, rumors persisted. And a few students, enough to be an annoyance, returned from Onyx as full converts. They would tell how the glyphs had imparted to them a special inspiration. And how they were certain, because of this special inspiration, that they were about to craft a monumental spell, one that could change the world.

As no such spell ever materialized, I was happy to focus on my studies and ignore all the hullaballoo. But then I met Celia.

In truth, I met her paintings first. I had gone down to the annual campus art show and found myself mesmerized by a set of mournful landscapes. Nothing about them suggested spell-craft. Nothing in them moved or twinkled or morphed into something new as you took them in. And yet, try as I might, I could not take my eyes off of the paintings until a deep sorrow rose within me and I wept. A woman approached and I hurried to wipe my eyes, embarrassed by my emotional outburst. When I turned to meet her eye, she gave a sympathetic smile.

"It's the damnedest thing," I said. "There's no spell on these paintings. They seem to belong in a mundane gallery."

"And yet?" she asked.

"And yet they've done something to me. As if something has been released that I didn't know was bottled up."

The woman nodded. "There's no spell cast on the painting because the painting is the spell," she said. "You spell-writers don't cast spells on top of the incantations you write, do you?"

I had never considered such an idea. All the spell-paintings I had ever seen were painted with the idea that certain incantations, usually ones that would animate the painting, would be cast on top.

"And what is the spell painted here?" I asked, pointing to the landscapes.

"I call it, 'Unearthing Sorrow'."

"That's genius," I said.

She smiled her true smile then, the one that lit up her face, the room, and, I was certain, the whole world. By some miracle, she took a fancy to me as well, and we fell under that kind of love spell which remains a mystery to cast; the one from which there is no cure but for one or both hearts to be torn asunder.

Our studies kept us busy in the day, but every evening we'd meet up to take long walks around the campus. During one of those moonlit strolls, Celia confessed that she had visited the glyphs in Onyx and felt the presence of her mother in the caves. She told me how, when she was still in her adolescence, her widowed mother had turned down a marriage proposal from a wealthy textile merchant. For years Celia had resented her for not wedding the merchant, blaming all the family's woes and poverty on her mother's pride. Until, finally, after the death of her younger sister from the crimson cough, Celia released a fit of rage on her mother, who had passed out of the world that very night.

"I have told myself a thousand times that my words didn't end her life," Celia said. "The fever did that. But I am always replaying those horrible last words I spoke to her. Standing next to the glyphs, I felt her presence. It was as if she were standing just behind the cave wall. And it seemed I had a chance to take those words back. I did and I told her —"

Her words caught in her mouth and she cried. I realized why Celia's paintings had worked so well on me. We shared a similar grief.

"And you saw an apparition in the caves? You saw your mother?" I asked.

"I felt her," she said. "It was as if the caves were commiserating with my grief."

"And did she hear you?" I asked, my heart in my throat.

"I don't know. But it helped to say the words out loud. To … allow them. I can't explain it. You have to go, Ben. You have to know them for yourself."

So, late in the summer, I boarded a zeppelin and floated over the North Sea to a shore of stark white sand and craggy black rock. Beyond the shore, a city rose, culminating in the gleaming white dome of the Onyxian Parliament sitting high on a hill.

I dropped my bag off at a ramshackle inn next to the southern docks and set off for the glyphs. They were not hard to find, as there was a steady stream of tourists heading to and from them. I followed the crowd down a winding path that ran along the cliffs facing the shore. Eventually, the path veered left and sloped down into the wide entrance of a cave. I had to brace myself as a strong and constant ocean breeze rushed past me and down into the cool mouth of the cave.

There was no need for a lantern, as there were so many lantern-wielding tourists already inside. In less than a half an hour I had made my way to the glyphs, which were in a small chamber off the main path. They seemed no more than geological anomalies, odd-looking white striations set in a black cave wall. I held the palm of my hand against them, as I saw some other tourists doing, and felt nothing. I returned to my inn dismayed that I had not felt even the slightest fraction of magic. But that night, I had a dream. The dream. The one that had plagued me since I was a child.

It was always the same: the dream began with a cruel reenactment of the worst day of my life – the day I decided to read "Colonel Bellington's Compendium of Spell-forms" instead of watching over my younger brother, Arthur. I was twelve and he was a capable five years old, but my mother still insisted I go with him whenever he wanted to swim. I sat under an apple tree as he flew into the water, and lost myself in the compendium.

"Come play, Ben!" he yelled out, splashing in the water. "Novels are boring."

"It's not a novel," I said. "It's a compendium of spells."

"Is there a spell to make me a shark?"

"These aren't for casting. They're just examples."

"You should read how to do fun stuff! You should learn how to make mud puddles when there's no rain. Or a spell that can turn me into a shark."

I don't know what he said after that because I began to ignore him. I became lost in the book and didn't look up from the page until I heard my father's cries. He had come in from the fields to wash in the pond and found Arthur in the lily-pads, floating blue.

From there, the dream departed from true events. I would descend into the pond, not to save Arthur, but to speak to him, to beg his forgiveness. My words would float away, a stream of shining bubbles racing to the surface, while Arthur looked on, his face blank, his eyes dead. And this scene would play out for an eternity until I awoke.

That night in Onyx, my dream was so vivid that I awoke choking, the taste of pond water still in my mouth. I was uncomfortably hot, sweating even after pulling off the sheets of my bed. I put on my boots and stepped outside, but the slight breeze coming off the shore gave no relief. I heard a chirp from above and looked to see a cloud of bats, their black wings barely visible against the midnight sky. They dove into the cliffs and I knew they must be following that chill current of wind that never stopped flowing into the caves. I had to join them, to find cool respite in the womb of the earth, and I hurried toward the caves, certain they were the only cure for my fever.

Still in my night clothes, with only the light of my single lantern, I descended into the caverns as the wind whipped around me. I felt a strange joy, as if being welcomed home after a long voyage, and could not keep myself from smiling. The caves should have been impossible to navigate in so little light, but I could not seem to take a wrong step. I somehow knew my way as if I were in my childhood home. When I came to the glyphs, my fever broke and a chill went through me. I had an odd sensation that Arthur was in the cave somewhere nearby. I spoke his name and waited for an answer.

A sudden gust of wind caught me off guard and I lost my balance. I dropped my lantern as I fell and, with a loud clang, all went black. At first, the darkness of the cave was nothing but a void, but as I scrambled to find my lantern, shapes began to fill in the void. There was an apple tree and below it a familiar book with a red cover. Beyond, I saw lush green grasses growing tall around a wide pond. Arthur came storming out of the water, his lanky limbs glittering in the afternoon sun. His mouth moved as if he were speaking but I couldn't hear him.

"Arthur!" I yelled and scrambled to my feet.

Urgently, he pointed behind me. I turned to see the red book beneath the apple tree flying toward me. It hovered in the air before me and opened itself. Its pages were blank, but as I peered into the book, a spell began to write itself. My heart swelled as I felt this must be a spell made especially for me, a spell that would allow me to speak with my brother, to finally beg his forgiveness and bring peace to both our hearts. I tried to read what was written but it was all in gibberish. I turned back to Arthur and saw a vast canyon of darkness had fallen between us.

"I'm sorry!" I yelled out. "I'm sorry! Can you hear me?"

But as I spoke, he dissolved into the darkness. I ran forward to find him as if there were a great stretch of space ahead of me and not a wall of stone. My head slammed against the hard rock and it felt as if I'd been sucker-punched by a prizefighter. I dropped to the ground and held my throbbing head until the pain dulled. As I did, the cave winds started back up and I could not stop shivering.

"Please," I said. "Please come back."

"Gotta come in the spring," a voice said. There was a flicker of yellow light and I made out a puffy-faced man sitting on the floor of the cave, his back against the glyph wall. He was holding a match and using it to light my lantern. He glared at me with hollow eyes, made a move to get up, decided he was too drunk for that and leaned once more against the wall.

"In the spring," he spat out. "Hasn't anybody told you! They ain't at their full power until the spring, dammit."

"Who are you?" I asked.

"That's not important. What the glyphs say, that's what's important. That's all that matters, isn't it?" he said "But you fools keep coming at the wrong time. Say it, then. You'll come back in the spring."

"I'll come back in the spring," I said.

"Good man. Now leave," he said thrusting the lantern into my hand. When I hesitated he yelled out "Get the hell out of here!"

He grew angrier, shouting various profanities until I fled back up to the surface. I was sure he was mad, but at the moment, madness made a great deal of sense. I took his advice to heart and promised myself to return in the spring.

On the zeppelin flight home, as I floated further from the glyphs, I could only think of Arthur in the caves and how he had nearly spoken to me. I decided I would devote my life to deciphering the spell I had not been able to read in that floating red book, that no matter how impossible a task it seemed, I would devise a spell to speak with the dead.

I returned to Silver Forge brimming with faith and optimism, happy to join the ranks of the true-believers. I asked Celia if she would go to Onyx with me once we had our degrees.

"Is this a proposal?" she asked.

"Dammitall, I think it is," I said.

I had no ring to present, but she didn't mind. She painted thin black bands on each of our ring fingers, and, together, we cast a spell to make the ink permanent. We graduated in the fall, exchanged vows, slid silver rings over our painted ones, and promptly sailed to Onyx.

The strangest thing about the island was not the spell crafting or the seclusion or even the odd political corruption of a city whose main export was sorcery, but the fact that so many tolerated the torment of its winter. In the dead of an Onyx winter, you despised yourself for staying, but you couldn't get out. By then, hardly any boat would chance the ice surrounding the island, nor any zeppelin take on the near-constant storms.

Each autumn, when the frigid winds began to blow, most of the island's residents would take the last ferries of the season back to the mainland, and of course, the rich would book flights to the sunny beaches of Zephyr's Banks. But Celia and I, along with all the other artists, would stay.

We stayed because only an Onyx winter could make you fully know its spring. Come visit with the tourists in the warm months and you would write home about how beautiful it was. "Oh, cousin Meredith, you must come to see the sparkling white beaches. And the old prince's castle on the precipice by moonlight. And the tulips blooming in all the colors of the rainbow!"

All fine and well, but if you wanted to know why the artists were here, you had to survive the winter. Then, when spring finally emerged, you would know her properly as your savior. Born again, you would kiss her feet, joyous to be swallowed in her ever-blooming ecstasy. And in this state you would have your best chance with the glyphs.

In the midst of that first winter, with frost on our breath even as a fire roared in our hearth, Celia and I decided we'd leave Onyx before another one came to pass. But in the spring, we went down into the caves, set our hands on the glyphs, and returned to the surface with our minds abuzz with inspiration. We strolled through the hills of blooming wildflowers as sand swirled on the beaches and waves lazily collapsed on the shore and we agreed we'd live in Onyx all the days of our lives.

When I had laid my hands on the glyphs that first spring I did not see Arthur, but heard his voice in my head, faintly humming his favorite lullaby. All the lyrics came back to me and it occurred to me they could be turned into a stellar sleeping spell. I decided this must be the first step in devising a spell to speak with the dead. I would combine an intense sleeping spell with one that could summon the deceased. And in this way, I would bring the living closer to death while luring the deceased closer to life. And there in the space between worlds, the living and the dead could commune. Did it bother me that I had no idea how to cast a spell on the deceased? That there was no precedent for it whatsoever? Not in the least. Standing before the glyphs, I had faith the details would iron themselves out. But when I sat down at home to begin writing, all my ideas became confused and impossible. What seemed rational in the caves, was absurdity anywhere else.

Meanwhile, Celia had felt moved to honor her mother and began a painting of her childhood home. She played with light in a new way and the painting was like a breath of fresh air for the soul. For a time, it was a joy to have that painting in our home, but Celia was never satisfied with it. She could not leave it alone. She painted over her work many times as spring became summer until the composition became disjointed and the only feeling it conjured was confusion.

We spent five years that way, cursing the winters, exalting the springs, and spending the months in between telling ourselves our big break-through was just around the corner.

I found work as a typesetter and Celia waited tables and we tried our best to make a name for ourselves as spell-crafters on an island teeming with people attempting to do exactly the same.

We had some mild successes. I had a knack for writing tawdry love spells which I published under a pen name. Most of them were dirt cheap, wore off too quickly, and had dubious effects, but love spells were in such demand, they could always sell. Celia would go down to the boardwalk and sell paintings to tourists of stars that would actually twinkle in night skies and suns that set before your very eyes. It was enough to keep us at our craft, but not enough to pay the bills.

By the fifth year, up to our necks in debt and without a break in sight, Celia made her case that we ought to leave.

"I'm stuck, Ben," she said. "It doesn't matter if I paint a carnival or a funeral. All my paintings are about my mother. I thought moving here, feeling my mother in the caves, would help me heal, but it's only made me fixated on her deathbed. I can't stand it anymore."

I had to admit that we were spinning our wheels, and wondered if the glyphs had ever been on our side. I began to think perhaps it was all some kind of cosmic joke and the caves were feeding off our frustrations. I could still sense Arthur when I stood before the glyphs, but I never had a vision as intense as my first trip. And despite a great deal of study, I had come no closer to writing a spell to speak with the dead. I asked Celia for a few weeks to mull over the idea of leaving the island for good. And while I did, winter came early. It came hard, choking the streets in snow and ice. The whole city shut down for months. Celia and I spent a great deal of time huddled by our fire, talking over the future. How we would move back to Silver Forge where the weather was mild, where rent was cheap and where spell-crafters like us could easily find work tutoring students. And then one morning I woke with a fever, retching from the taste of pond water in my mouth.

"Ben, don't be a moron," Celia said when she saw me putting on my boots. "There's still snow on the ground." Her auburn hair was pulled back and her smock was splattered in violet specks of paint. She had woken early and had begun painting before we'd even made coffee.

I put two layers of sweaters on and said, "There's been a shift. Spring is here. I've never felt it so strong. You feel it too, don't you?"

"I did feel it," she said. "I woke inspired." She sighed and wiped her forehead, smearing purple paint across it. "I had a vision of hope."

I examined her painting. It was the landscape just outside our window. There were the city rooftops, all in shadow, and beyond, the low rolling hills covered in snow. Above the hills, Celia had painted a lone seagull. I thought he might drop out of the pale blue sky at any moment out of sheer despair.

"How do you feel?" she asked.

"Heavy," I said.

She slammed her paintbrush down on the easel. "I give up," she said. "I can't escape my mother, or rather, my insufferable self-pity. I'm a one-trick pony. It's all despair and grief and sorrow and blah, blah, blah."

She turned to me, hands on her hips. "I think we ought to make a child."

"Right now?"

"Yes, please."

"You'd have a child as if you were casting a spell. As if there's some magic in it that will make you stop painting your mother."

She shrugged. "Why wouldn't it?"

I laughed. "Be serious. We can barely feed ourselves, Cee-Cee!"

"We're moving, remember? To a place where people like us are sought after. Where we aren't just another set of dreamers."

"Let's not put the cart before the horse. We'll move and then make a family."

I put on my cloak and poured what was left of the previous night's broth into a canteen.

"Where are you going?" she asked. "There's no way the shops are opening this early. I don't care how much we feel it's spring."

"I'm going to the glyphs."

"Moron! You'll slip on some black ice in those caves and that'll be the end of you."

"I have to go."

"Why?"

"Arthur told me."

Just before I awoke that morning Arthur had finally done something besides stare at me with his wretched dead eyes. When I had descended into the pond, he had turned to look behind him. There, instead of the usual sun-streaked murk of the pond, I had seen the glyphs, shining bright in the darkness.

Having heard this explanation, Celia turned to her painting and sighed. She addressed the canvas as if it were an old friend familiar with my nonsense.

"I can't argue with Arthur, can I?" she asked.

"I'm sorry," I said.

"Go then, moron. I very much hope you don't die."

I trudged through the snow toward what I thought should be the entrance of the caves, but the cliffs were still blanketed in snow. I sipped my broth and waited for the sun to rise. As it did, the snows shrank and little streams of icy water began to race toward the shores. Finally, a mass of snow toppled from the cliffs and, beyond it, I made out the dark maw of the cave entrance.

I lit my lantern and descended into the cave, but when I reached the entrance to the glyph chamber, I paused. Something was off. I stood a long while contemplating what it was until I realized there was no wind in the cave. And in the place of the rushing wind I could hear a low hum, a vibration I could feel in my bones. I had the distinct feeling there was someone waiting for me. I thought for sure I'd find that old drunk man sitting against the glyph wall, but when I stepped forward, I was alone.

As soon as I saw the glyphs, they began to move. They shifted, blurred, and melted into the cave wall. I was horrified that they might vanish for good. I tried to run to them, but darkness enveloped me. I flailed my arms and realized I was under water, floating in the pond behind my childhood home. I turned my head and there was Arthur, floating before me, only he was alive. I knew he was alive. And I knew I could reach out and bring him back. I knew we'd climb a tree and race for the highest branch. We'd catch frogs and drop them at the top of the hill so we could chase them back down into the pond. And we'd laugh at how he'd almost drowned.

I reached and pulled him to me, and as I did, I was pulled once more into myself. Alone, I stood in the cave, submerged not in water, but in a torrent of thought.

I had a clarity of mind like I'd never experienced before, or since. Parts of spells I had been mulling over for months began sliding into one another and making themselves whole. I sprinted out of the cave in a ruckus and burst forth into the sunlight surrounded by a cloud of black wings that screeched and fluttered into the pink evening sky.

"I have it!" I yelled. "I have it all!"

When I stormed through the door of our flat, I saw that Celia had destroyed the painting she'd been working on. It had been doused in scarab ether, a highly effective paint thinner. All the colors had melded together into a sick dripping brown. Celia was passed out in bed, her smock still on, our last bottle of wine lying empty in her arms. The myriad of burning thoughts shooting through my mind all fell away. The sight of Celia in such disarray stripped me of any other idea than to relieve her of her grief. Celia was the kindest, warmest person I knew, and it seemed a great injustice that she ought to carry the guilt of her mother's deathbed with her always.

Barely thinking, I sat down and wrote "Regret's Relief" for her. The spell allowed a person to forgive themselves, irrevocably, for what they most regretted. I had such a clarity of thought it was not hard to make scarab ether the only casting cost, and as soon as it was written, I cast "Regret" on my still sleeping Celia. I then turned back to my desk and began to write the spell that I felt was my destiny. A spell to speak with the dead.

I started off well enough, but halfway through, my writing became confused. I read over my work several times, trying to regain my train of thought until my eyelids grew heavy. Exhaustion overwhelmed me and I passed out on my writing table. I awoke shivering, the fire in our flat having gone out. I read the partially finished spell and it seemed as foreign as if another hand had written it. The clarity of the glyphs had fogged over.

The inspiration did not return, even when I went back down into the caves. It was as if the glyphs had given me the totality of their gift and the tap was now shut off. Still, every morning I would wake and force myself to attempt finishing the spell. Each morning would end with me pounding my fist on the writing table and burning all my failed work in the fire.

While my frustrations grew, Celia's abated. It took some time to see a change, and it was hard to say when exactly it took hold, but one day I knew it like I knew winter from spring. Her step was ever so faintly lighter, her sleep just a smidge deeper, and her smile, though I previously thought it impossible, became even brighter. Still, I watched her work closely. I had worried "Regret" would make her art suffer, that if she did not carry that certain pain, she couldn't infuse it into her art. And yet, the opposite was true. She now painted with more confidence and with a greater sense of purpose. Her grief was still there, but instead of wrestling with it, she embraced it and held it firm in her grasp.

People began swearing up and down that they felt an improvement in their health after visiting her exhibition. She leaned into this idea and found herself painting a sunrise that could ease a headache. All of Onyx came to see it. High Society took notice and began an onslaught of commissions she couldn't hope to keep up with.

By late spring, when parliament opened its door to the public, I was certain "Regret" had worked just as I had written it. I applied for patent approval and was immediately asked to present myself for questioning. Most of the patent committee agreed there had to be some sort of catch. That no spell, especially one that dealt with matters of the heart and mind, no matter how inspired, could be written that clean. I pointed out the spell could only be used once on each person, and they began to warm to its poetry. To test it, the head magistrate used the spell on herself. She wept, stamped my patent, left Onyx that very day, and never returned.

"Regret's Relief" was, however, deemed a protected spell that could not be sold to the public. Parliament feared the spell would be ill-used by the morally bankrupt, allowing degenerates to alleviate the weight of their conscience. Parliament would administer the spell only to those who seemed fit after thorough interviews. I agreed to their terms and received a lump sum of 500 dollars.

I paid off our outstanding debts and bought the finest pen and paper money could buy. I told myself I could finish "Commune with the Dead" if only my hand could glide more smoothly across the page. I never wrote so much trash in all my life as with that damned pen. Occasionally I'd stumble upon a functional spell, but nothing close to finishing "Commune." The best I crafted was an incantation to make mourners more talkative at their loved one's wake.

I also had to deny my constant urge to seek out the glyphs, allowing myself to descend only once per week. And though they never gave me a single clue on how to finish "Commune", I kept going until, at the peak of summer, the caves were shut down. When I arrived that afternoon, police guarded the entrance. I joined the other agitated glyph devotees as tempers flared until the coroner arrived and announced there had been a death in the caves. I stayed to watch the government spelunkers haul a body out and saw that it was the old drunk man from my first visit to the caves. Someone in the crowd wondered if he'd drunk himself to death.

"Glyph-sickness!" a woman yelled out. "They won't write that in the obituary, but it's the truth. Seen it too many times! Sonovabitch had a family and everything."

On my walk home I had to stop as my stomach clenched. I doubled over and vomited my lunch onto the grass. As I convulsed, I realized I resented the old drunk, then I despised him, and then I hated him with all my being. The bastard was more than half the reason I'd come to Onyx in the first place and now he was keeping me from my glyphs, keeping me from "Commune with the Dead", keeping me from Arthur. I thought I might have strangled the son of a bitch if he weren't already dead.

I returned home sweating and belligerent, to find Celia painting furiously. Our flat was covered with her finished work, every painting a sunrise, every one heartbreakingly beautiful. My temper cooled as I took in the landscapes and I wondered at how I could have been so angry about the death of a stranger.

Celia rushed to me, slapping zeppelin tickets in one hand and a glass of bubbly in the other. The tickets were for Zephyr's Bank.

"How much did this cost?" I asked.

"The Dome, Ben! I'm in the Dome!"

She had won a showing at the Obsidian Dome, at the time the most prestigious gallery in the hemisphere. To celebrate, she demanded we go on vacation. As it turned out, she'd been stowing cash in secret to surprise me. She insisted we go all out and rent a cottage on Zephyr's Bank. As there seemed no option to disagree, I told myself it was providence. I could take a break from the glyphs, and perhaps gain a new perspective on "Commune with the Dead."

It was while we were in Zephyr's Bank that the Patent Committee of the Onyxian Parliament let "Regret's Relief" be known to the public, writing at length about its potentials in The Northwestern Journal of Incantation. Word spread through Zephyr quickly until Celia came to dinner with her eyes brimming over with tears.

"Ben," she said, "did you cast it on me?" The truth of it was so plain, I couldn't hope to lie. I confessed. She held me and cried and thanked me. I apologized for casting the spell on her without her consent. She said she didn't care. And then she pled for me to cast it on myself.

"It wouldn't work the same," I said. "I have too many regrets."

"Look at you. Every night I hear you gasping and groaning. You haven't had an honest night's sleep in months. And your days are spent working on this cursed spell that clearly doesn't want to be written. This has to stop, Ben."

Leaving Onyx had not, as I'd hoped, alleviated my desire for the glyphs. I woke several times each night, always in a sweat and gasping for air. I would spend most of my days sitting on the beach with my journal and pen, facing the direction of Onyx, sometimes writing, but mostly staring out at the sea. In the face of insurmountable evidence against my mental well-being, I had no choice but to lie.

"I'm fine," I said. "Creating a spell so immense has put me in a state of unrest, but there will be an end."

The lie sounded good and I decided to believe it myself. "Every day," I said, "I come closer to finishing my work."

"Then let's make a child," Celia said. "What are we waiting for? Poverty is no longer an excuse. People will throw money at you and me alike, just to hear us pontificate on the arts."

"We're on our way up, Celia. Children would only slow us down."

"I want a child, Ben."

"Soon."

"Why not now?"

"Let art be your child!"

She struck me then. Celia, who barely had the nerve to smack a gnat, made the full brunt of her painter's hand known to me.

"Don't make this about me," she said. "It's about you. It's about Arthur."

We did not speak the rest of that day, nor the next, which was our final day of the vacation. We did, however, follow through on our plan to picnic for dinner. We had yet to observe the evening ritual of the crabs coming into the bay, and neither of us wanted to miss it. We sat on the beach in silence as the crab's mating ritual set the night shore aglow in a humming violet bioluminescence. The full moon hung low, shining bright. It pulled at the womb of the earth and I felt that gravity shoot through my soul. For a fleeting moment, I saw myself making a family with Celia. She must have seen it in my eye because she said, "I deserve it, Ben. We deserve it."

She was lying on the bed of bluegrass, just off the sand, in an ivory gown bathed in starlight. The King of Fairies might have mistaken her for his queen. I played the part of an ass and did nothing about it. Instead, I looked out over the bay, and even though I knew it was impossible, I decided I could see the shores of Onyx on the horizon.

In the morning, as I was packing my things for the return, Celia laid her hand on mine.

"Let's stay," she said.

I froze and waited for her to go on, but she only stared at me steadfast and pitying.

"I have to return," I said.

"That island is making you sick, Ben. We should be the happiest we've ever been, but you're a mess. My sister is a day's train ride away in Silver Forge. Let's go for a visit."

I allowed myself to consider not returning to Onyx and my stomach turned itself over. Bile rose in my throat.

"This is how you repay me?" I asked. "I release you from the torment of your mother and now you'd stop me from writing my masterpiece?"

"I'm going to Silver Forge," she said. "And I want you to come with me. What I'm not going to do is watch you torture yourself when you could simply cast 'Regret' on yourself and be free from Arthur."

"You mean I should leave him behind. Abandon him."

"He's gone, Ben."

"Go, then. Go to Silver Forge and find some poor schmuck and make all the babies you want."

She didn't dignify my attack with a response. She only packed her things, told me to come to Silver Forge when I was ready, and left on the next train. I told myself it was all for the best. That our paths had diverged. We were getting in the way of each other's happiness.

When I returned to Onyx I marched straight for the caves, only to find the entrance still boarded over. Only now there was a notice glued to the boards announcing that another poor soul had died in the caves and, until thorough investigations could be completed, the caves were closed indefinitely.

Celia wrote asking me to send her painting supplies, and a few weeks later, she wrote again asking for her wardrobe.

Several months after that, she asked for the rest of her things. In each letter she would describe the many well-paying jobs I could take on in Silver Forge and how she thought she could set up her own school for spell-painting. I shipped her things off and responded to her letters by repeating the lie I now held most dear: that I was oh so very close to finishing my work and that I would be along soon.

Eventually, the flat was void of most all her things and I realized how little I had. There was my writing table, the bed, the dresser of clothes. They all stared at me like idiot friends.

"All for the best," they said. "Now you're free to get some real work done."

Winter came and I spent it alone in a flat that was too empty and in dreams that were too real. There were a few dark days in the dead of winter where I convinced myself the flat was the afterlife, a purgatory made up special for me.

When spring returned and I was able to go out and meet with people again, I gained back some sanity. I wrote a letter to Celia telling her I was ready to have children. That I was going to write a book of love spells. That I was done with the glyphs and "Commune with the Dead" for good. I took it to the post office and was about to drop it into the mail bin when a vision came to me. I saw a host of my own children perishing as they fell off of roofs, tripped down stairs, got run over by trains, and drowned in ponds while I sat hunched over my writing desk. I took the letter home and fed it to the fire.

I began taking sleeping draughts to keep my dreams at bay and quickly became addicted to them. When those became too expensive, I turned to hard liquor. I lost my typesetting job and was booted from the flat after missing half a year's rent. I washed dishes for The Mermaid's Tale and the owner let me stay in his attic. I told myself I was waiting for a sign from the glyphs, or Arthur, or something I could not name.

When the ferries once more declared they had two weeks left before they closed for the winter, I wept. I was a failure, and a drunk to boot. I felt myself a coward as well, terrified of another winter in Onyx, of what it might do to my mind. I bought a ferry ticket for Silver Forge. I had an idea I would search out Celia and beg her forgiveness, but as the ship left the dock, I rushed off, leaping back to the shore.

"Now," I told myself. "Now that you've given up all you have. Now that you've shown the glyphs how serious you are, they will deliver you!"

I stumbled through the first snow flurries of the year, my veins coursing with more booze than blood. I brought a hammer with me and the last I remember was many failed attempts to pry the boards off the cave entrance.

When I came to, I was lying on a hospital bed. Celia stood over me. Her belly was round with child and her hair was shorter but shone brighter. She had dark circles under her eyes and I could tell that she had been crying.

"Dammitall," I said. "You've got to leave. I don't want you to see me like this."

"Too late," she said, and she laid her hand on mine. I saw her silver wedding band was gone, but the one of black ink remained.

"You shouldn't be here," I said. "Winter will come. You'll be stranded."

"You're right," she said. "I have tickets to return to Silver Forge tomorrow morning. So buck up and show these nurses you can walk out of here."

I found I could stand on my own, and I put on my best show for the nurses. Celia signed me out of the hospital and escorted me down to Angler's Brewery by the piers. She had sold a painting to the owner recently and wanted me to see it. So we sat by the Angler's hearth and took in her work, hung over the mantel.

The painting was of our flat, back when we'd both inhabited it. I waited until the cordial I'd ordered was finished before I took my eyes off the painting and steadied them on Celia.

"I feel no change," I said. "I fear your painting's a dud."

"I think you should write some spells for Arthur."

"That's what I've been trying to do."

"No. You've been trying to write something for yourself. Write something for Arthur."

I could see she was watching me, the way I had once watched her. I looked at the painting again and a weight lifted. A key turned. A frost on my heart shook free.

She laughed and wept at the same time. "I'm sorry it took so long to paint. You're a stubborn little moron, so it had to be just so."

"What is it? Did you somehow paint 'Regret's Relief?'"

"No. I went with a different approach."

"What then?"

She smiled. "A love spell."

"And whom will I fall in love with?"

"Yourself. You'll love yourself as much as I did. As much as I do. And there's nothing you can do about it, moron."

She sat back in her chair, arms crossed, beaming.

I thought of saying "Damn you to hell," but all that came out was, "Thank you, Celia."

She wiped her eyes, took a deep breath, and stared at the ring of ink on her left hand.

"Help me cast this off?" she asked.

"Maybe I won't."

"You will."

"Why?"

"Because you love me."

We spoke the spell together and I watched as the ink slowly faded away from both our hands.

We shared one glass of wine and I let her go home. I sat in Angler's, ordered a coffee, paper, and an ink-pot. I scribbled out a spell I called "Puddle Prisms" that made mud puddles that shone with all the colors of the rainbow. I used all my knowledge of shadows and light to make an illusion wherein ordinary fish would momentarily look like great big sharks. And then I wrote another spell for Arthur, and another, and as I wrote I felt Arthur's spirit rise within me and go swimming across the page.

See Travis Wade Beaty's story "Regret's Relief" online at Metaphorosis.
If you liked it, leave a comment. Authors love that!
Remember to subscribe to our e-mail updates so you'll know when new stories are posted.

About the story

I started writing "Regret's Relief" while visiting Paris and reading *A Moveable Feast* by Ernest Hemingway. The initial idea was to go to that Paris of Hemingway and Picasso and Gertrude Stein etc., but imagine the art they were trying to create was magic. I enjoyed delving into the idea of a frustrated spell-crafter, so the story I wrote originally was a lot about that. Eventually, as I revised the story, it became influenced by my own experiences of living in Los Angeles in my 20s and struggling to make a career out of acting.

Also, seasons were on my mind a great deal after having moved to Washington, DC after seven years in Los Angeles. I experienced the change of seasons growing up in Indiana, but LA was void of that passage from dead winter into vibrant spring. Experiencing that first spring in DC with all the cherry blossoms was quite a spiritual experience for me. So I was eager to put that feeling into a story.

A question for the author

Q: Do you often include children in your stories? What role do they play?

A: I include children in my stories fairly often. Children are full of hope and are themselves a kind of manifestation of hope. So I like to see how cynical or hard-hearted adult characters might respond to being confronted with that kind of limitless optimism of a child.

There's also that strong desire to protect children which can inspire a lot of fear. And letting a kid down can really haunt a person. So as a parent, I spend a lot of time thinking about that push and pull between hope and fear and all the doubts between.

About the author

Travis Wade Beaty grew up in Northern Indiana, spent a good deal of his twenties in Los Angeles, and now resides in Washington, DC. While he's had a great many jobs, his favorites have included acting, teaching, and being a stay-at-home dad to two girls and three cats.

@TravisWBeaty

Pre-triage

Joe Prosit

As of today, I'm a human crumple-zone. I saw to that myself. The highway network will see my car and label me the perfect impact absorber.

There was a time I thought I had things all figured out. I had a good job. I had plans. Ambitions. Goals. A house of cards sent toppling down when they pulled my job out from underneath me. My severance package, nothing more than a handshake and an escort out the door, told me exactly what I was worth. It was a rough year. A rough couple of years.

I figured it out, though – how to rebuild that card house into something the system would value. I married a doctor.

Her name was Linda. She had everything. A beautiful face. Gorgeous eyes. Wavy brown hair. Long legs and a knock-out body. A great fashion sense too; I got a lot of advice on picking out her clothes and accessories before I bought them for her. Her physical presence was the easy part. I built that from old car parts and a suede recliner I had in the garage. But she had a great personality too. I spent hours creating her digital footprint and integrating it into her physical body via her cellphone and the biometrics I gave her. She wasn't just beautiful to my eyes. When I helped her turn on her phone, the network saw her face and her retinas, and felt her 3D printed thumb prints the same as I did. But Linda went beyond just biometrics. According to her records, she worked the ER at a Level 1 Trauma hospital, donated to charities, and coached our son's soccer team. She was a great mother to all three of our kids.

Luke, Jeremy, Abigail... They had lives too. I built them in the garage and integrated them into the network not long after Linda and I got together. They were enrolled in sports, wore cool clothes, had friends online, and streamed the newest hip music. Their faked school records weren't all straight A's, but they worked hard and really made an effort. So what if maybe they spent a little too much time on their phones playing games and streaming videos? I knew the metrics the network used to quantify the value of their lives, so I maxed theirs out. As far as the system could tell, we were the perfect family. Worth saving.

I think it all went to hell the moment we trusted the computers to drive for us.

See, back then, when I was working and all I had was my job, I was a highway systems engineer. I did the final coding on tying the whole highway network together. There was a lot of work to be done during the months before launch day. A lot of overtime. That was when I came across the "pre-triage" protocol. Never heard of pre-triage? Never heard of triage? It's French, meaning "to sort".

Imagine for a moment, being a paramedic back when humans drove cars.

You come upon a wreck and you and your partner have ten patients. Three are fine. Bumps and bruises. Three others are flat-lined dead. Of the remaining four, two are so close to dying there is only a slim chance you could save either one. The other two you know you can save, but only if you give them all your attention. Whom do you treat? The two who have the best chance of being saved, right? You'd play God and you would decide, these people will live and these people will die. That's triage.

It's no different nowadays, only we programmed the network to decide instead of the paramedics. And the network chooses before the first collision ever takes place. Say a deer jumps out on the road. As soon as it's detected, the network knows that the thing that should not happen is about to happen: there's going to be a wreck. A nasty one too. A pile-up. People will surely die. So what does it do? Pre-triage. Some cars become impact absorbers while others are spared. It becomes a numbers game. This car has five passengers. This car has one. This car is carrying a happy family and a Nobel Prize winner. This car is carrying a single out-of-work engineer with a drinking problem. These people live. This one dies. For the good of others, your car just might decide that you should die. That's pre-triage.

So my plan began as a way to stay safe on the highway. As the family grew, it was only natural for the network to see how valuable we were. Instead of being a lone washed-up programmer clinging to the bottle, I was a husband and a father. I was a good one, too. My wife was a respected doctor, advanced in her field. Our kids had real potential; I poured hours of attention into them, making sure they'd make the most of it. In the end, we had a measurable, quantifiable, benefit to society. Most people wouldn't recognize it at first glance, but I saw how special my family was, and the network saw it too. It was right. This was about more than just me staying alive on the highway; it was about raising a family that trusted and needed me, regardless how some bank of computers scored the value of our lives.

Between you and me, by the morning we met, I'd stopped worrying about highway safety. I was enjoying spending time with my family during aimless rides along the highway. The network was performing flawlessly. Road travel was more efficient than ever before. More cars on the road. Higher speeds. Shorter commutes. Highway fatalities had dropped to ninety five percent. And the network enjoyed a near perfect customer satisfaction rating. By April fifth, 2025, I didn't worry about fifty car pile-ups anymore. Nobody did.

I read the police report. It was an unsecured load that started the accident that morning. Some trucker didn't inspect his tie-downs before hitting the road. It's always human error, whenever you ask us engineers. A load of cinder blocks fell off his truck. The blocks brought the first vehicle to an "unanticipated spontaneous halt".

The next ten cars were "impact absorbers". Nothing could be done about that. You were in car eleven. I was in car twelve. It was up to the network to pre-triage us correctly.

It seems like just yesterday. I heard the screeching brakes and the ten smashes like rhythmic thunderclaps coming closer and closer to me and my family. I was scared. I grabbed Linda to hold her back, to keep her safe from the collision I knew was coming. I reached out to little Abigail, praying to god I'd put the car seat in right. You know how they say only one in ten car seats are installed correctly? That's all I could think about as I waited for the next thunderclap to hit my family.

I wasn't thinking about your family.

The thunderclap came. No flash-to-bang delay. Just one big crash. Metal twisted and bent. Tiny bits of glass filled the air. I swear I could hear the boys screaming.

We hit your car still going seventy miles per hour. The car behind us hit us going forty. The network, in all the infinite wisdom we gave it, decided to save me and my family. When the impacts had been absorbed, when the tires stopped squealing, when the glass and bits of metal settled on the blacktop, when the frame of your car collapsed and mine remained rigid, we ended up okay. Linda was scared, but not injured. The boys were crying, and I was happy to hear it. It meant they were still in one piece, thank God. Abigail, I thought maybe she was hurt, she was so quiet. Panicked, I unbuckled and crawled over the seats to see inside her car seat.

And there she was, pretty as an angel, as healthy and happy as the day I built her from a baby doll, an old laptop, and steel springs. My relief was infinite. I cried and held them all close. I can't say how long we stayed in the car, just holding each other and thanking God we'd made it through okay. It wasn't until the rescue crews opened our door with the jaws-of-life that I got out and saw the rest of the accident.

They checked me out, saw I was okay, were confused about my family, but triaged them as not needing any medical attention. Then they went to your car.

I was standing on the shoulder of the road when they extricated you and your fiancée. You were unconscious but mumbling her name. That's how I know it. Abby. That's what me and Linda called our baby for short. Abby.

When they pulled her out, your Abby, she came out like Jell-O from a mold. Loose, like there were no bones left in her body. Blood everywhere. Her blonde hair was matted and stained dark. There was no sentience in her movements. Her limbs and head went where the firemen moved them or where gravity pulled them. There was no will left in her body. No life. I'm glad you weren't awake to see it. I can't get the image out of my head.

I'm sorry.

I can't look at my family the same way after that day. I can't look them in the eyes. I'm too ashamed of myself. They're too beautiful and I'm too...

I bet your Abby was beautiful too. Before the accident.

I'm sending this to let you know I deactivated the sensors in my car. I'm not carrying any electronic devices. Understand that I knew exactly what I was doing when I first put my family into a car, and I know exactly what I'm doing now. Now, when I drive, the network will see my car as being empty, like I'm not even there. It will see me for exactly what I'm worth: A crumple zone. An impact absorber.

I took your fiancée from you. I took all the potential you had for a family. So I'm sending you mine. They're in a car now, heading to your home over at 2600 Juniper Street. I got your address from the police report. I hope you don't mind. Linda is a great partner. The boys...

they're just amazing kids; I know you'll think so too after spending some time with them. And my Abigail. I took your Abby from you. I hope mine fills that hole, even just a little bit. Think of her as your Abby reborn. She's my gift to you.

I'm going out on the road now. I got plenty of fuel and plenty of booze to keep me on the highway for a while. I figure eventually the network will use me for what I'm worth. I trust it to administer justice. I have faith in it now.

That's all I got to say I guess. Just that I'm sorry. That, and please take good care of my family.

See Joe Prosit's story "Pre-Triage" online at Metaphorosis.
If you liked it, leave a comment. Authors love that!
Remember to subscribe to our e-mail updates so you'll know when new stories are posted.

About the story

Some stories fall right into my lap. This one was gifted to me one day when a buddy and I were driving down the road and the topic of self-driving cars came up. I mentioned how the roads will be safer and people can spend their time better. He said "All that's great, until the day your car decides to kill you." That was all he said, but after that the story wrote itself.

A question for the author

Q: Do you write with a particular audience in mind?

A: I don't write for any particular reader in mind. I guess I'm self-serving in the way that, if I enjoy the story, if I think it's creepy or compelling or speaks to me, then I write it. When other people connect, it makes it all the more satisfying because it's natural and unforced. Nothing is contrived.

About the author

Joe Prosit writes sci-fi, horror, and psycho fiction. He lives with his wife and kids in the Brainerd Lakes Area of northern Minnesota. If you're an adept stalker, you can find him on one of the many lakes and rivers or lost deep inside the Great North Woods. Or you can just find him on the internet at JoeProsit.com and on Twitter.

@JoeProsit

A Witch's Guide to Mushrooms and Toadstools

Hannah Hulbert

I kick my way through the decomposing leaves and they cling to my skirts. Others flit around me on the dying breath of summer, adding to the carpet that already comes up to my ankle. The only sound is the titter of thrushes and the distant drone of cattle. The track lies far behind me. I remind myself that I like being alone. That the forest is my ally. But I shiver anyway and quicken my pace.

I spot a likely tree and climb the bank towards it. Broad, lobed leaves, brown and sparse. Broad trunk, shaggy with lichen. An oak. I stoop to examine the base, digging Granny's notebook out of my pocket.

Breast-Feather

A frilly fungus that grows at the foot of hardwood trees. Pale, tongue-like brackets fork out from a central stem, supporting a wrinkled, leathery brown fruitbody. Mousey smell. Young mushrooms form a delicate creamy ruffle and are delicious fried in butter. Specimens darken with age as they gain potency.

Her archaic looped handwriting is unlike my own spidery scrawl. I hold up the image she inked in beside the description, alive with the affection she had for nature, painstakingly studied and preserved on the page for whoever inherited the cottage and the duties she left behind her. For me. I close my eyes and shake my head, scattering the emotions rising up, threatening to cloud my eyes and judgement.

I compare the image with the mushroom sprouting from the tree. This is definitely the one, and nicely matured. A citadel of undulating rooftops fit for fae kings and queens, Granny told me when I was small. I imagine I am a giant come to destroy their home as I slice a handful away from the bark with my pocket knife.

I wrap it in a cloth and head back towards the cottage, regretting not the destruction, but the bitter aftertaste of the sweet memory.

I set the mushroom on the kitchen windowsill to dry and the cast iron kettle on top of the stove to boil. While I wait, I perch on the wooden stool next to Granny's empty rocking chair, just like I always did and never managed to shake the habit of doing. I turn back to the Breast-Feather entry.

Dry for one moon until thin and tough, then grind into a fine powder. Use two teaspoons-full with nettle and black cohosh to brew a tea. Have the woman who longs for a child drink a cup every morning with breakfast and every evening before bed. Have her leave an offering of ripe fruit beside the tree from which the mushroom came with a prayer that the spirits will look favourably upon her.

Granny always used to say that everything we need is already in the world around us. I used to feel the same, a bone-deep contentment, before she died. But the space she left in my world is too big to be filled. Instead I find ways to skirt the void and not fall into it.

The kettle whistles in a steamy crescendo and I rise to remove it. I will tell Cicely when I do my round of the village that her tea will be ready in a month. I picture the joy on the faces of her and her young husband. A joy Granny made possible, still touching the lives of our small community from beyond the grave. The shadow she still casts is a comfort to us all, yet the size of it fills me with dread. That I should be expected to fill that darkness with my own wavering light. My eyes well with tears again, and this time I do nothing to restrain them.

The fractal patterns of the season's first frost cover the window, earlier than I had expected. The silver shimmer of the lawn beyond is muted by mist. I pull on my boots and warmest cloak and push the door open, stepping into the cold.

The air is sharp in my throat when I inhale and my breath forms wispy clouds. All is still, with the exception of a flash of russet and an obnoxious burst of song as a robin wings past. The sparkling blades of grass crunch underfoot as I head towards the forest.

A sweet chestnut fell five years ago not far up the track that leads into the village and I trudge through banks of ice-laced leaves towards it. Granny always had high hopes for a crop of Winter Mushrooms here. I dutifully visited throughout the year, waiting for the fulfilment of her prophecy.

The wood crumbles into soft, damp fragments under gentle pressure from my fingertips. A whole host of liverworts and fungi adorn the length of the trunk. I keep my gaze fixed on the decomposing wood as I walk the length of it, searching.

And there they are. Winter Mushrooms. Granny's book comes out and I double check the description and sketch.

Winter Mushroom

The Winter Mushroom is a tan umbrella with edges rolling down and inwards. Its scales are dark. The adnexed gills below are whitish. The young stem is pale, but browns with age. Pick it from the base. The cap fits in your palm, cool and smooth.

I snap one from the decaying trunk and turn it over. The gills are the pages of an unreadable book. I stroke them and they spring back into place, fluttering as I leaf through them. The content is silvery spores, not words. I produce a string bag from a pocket and fill it. Granny was right, again.

Back at home, the kitchen embraces me with its residual warmth. I tug off my boots and hang my cloak by the door. I open the stove to stir the embers and add some coal. By the time I have washed and sliced three mushrooms the pan set atop the stove is glowing. I fry the sliced mushrooms in oil and save the rest of the harvest for Cicely.

I take down the tatty recipe book from the shelf and browse the handwritten entries as I sit down to my hot breakfast. The mushroom flesh is rich and meaty and firm between my teeth. The pages are speckled with grease in places and browned. I fold the corner of the page when I find it, so I can copy it out later.

Winter Mushroom broth

Boil a large pan of water. Add to it a dozen winter mushrooms (sliced), a large knob of ginger root (chopped), four cloves of garlic (crushed), an onion (diced) and a handful of thyme. Simmer until the mushrooms are tender and serve piping hot.

This broth is excellent for the expectant mother, to bolster both her health and that of the fledgling life she carries.

Granny's elegant letters blur into illegibility as my eyes fill with tears, unable to read her words. Unable to taste her soup again. Unable to sit down for a simple meal of mushrooms together. Now it falls to me to follow the directions, to teach Cicely how to prepare the soup as Granny once taught me, hoping to do both justice.

When I open my curtains, the last of the snow heaped at either side of the lane has finally melted away. I dress for cold weather but when I step outside I am engulfed in birdsong and warmth and I cannot help but smile.

A few optimistic snowdrops have ventured up through the lawn. I spot a pale pink circle under the apple tree and make a bee-line towards it. A fairy-ring of around twenty pretty mushrooms. I crouch to admire them. The cold air is pungent with salt and ammonia. I fish the book out of the pocket inside my cloak where it spent the entire winter.

Rose Parasol

The Rose Parasol grows in rings, an early herald of spring. They are beautiful *to behold, but they are deadly. Easily detected by the smell of sperm. Each umbonate cap is a delicate pink with silken streaks radiating from the hub. The stem is slender and a little paler than the cap. If you peek below, the gills are dove-grey.*

The Old Lore tells that Rose Parasol rings mark the perimeter of portals to other realms. If you have an individual in your care for whom your skill will not suffice, this is where they might bring their petition.

How many times did Granny lead me about the garden, teaching me the names and uses of the living things around us? How many stories of little-folk did she tell me, weaving magic out of the mundane? A magic that has faded. The power I wield is a poor shadow of what I knew Granny was capable of, back when I was small and she was a giant, invincible and eternal.

My nose tingles. I screw my lips tight together and step into the circle. And there I let out a sob, and beg wordlessly for meaning or guidance or comfort from the unanswering powers. I receive none of these, only a modicum of catharsis.

The Rose Parasols, or their descendants, last all through the spring.

They are where I bring Cicely when she bleeds at the beginning of the summer. She and I stand side by side at the perimeter, hand in hand. I have done all I can and offered my small, floundering words of condolence. This was the only other comfort I could think offer. The warmth of our entwined fingers and a place to vent at the empty sky.

She teeters on the edge of hope, knowing what the blood signifies yet refusing to believe it. I do not encourage her hope, knowing it is unfounded.

When it emerges, her grief is raw and spans universes. I hold mine quietly; a small, dark well that delves into the earth. It is easily concealed, but my sorrow for Cicely tugs at the cover I set over it. I clasp her hand a little tighter.

Cicely pulls away and moans as she steps over the perimeter, a mourning too great for words. I wait at the sideline, brimming with pity and self-pity. And the doubt. The dread that there is something I could have done or failed to do. And always the space in my life where Granny should have been, ensuring I fulfil my duties properly, reassuring me. My higher power.

I leave the cottage by the kitchen door, squelch across the waterlogged lawn, and climb the stile at the back of the garden. A thrush in the hazel clump fills the warm air with melody. Bumblebees drone amid the tiny white flowers on the bramble as I step down into the paddock.

Nellie the old grey donkey is nowhere to be seen, but she has left plenty of heaps of manure. I wade through the glistening waves of grass, examining each island of dung, until I find the mushrooms I am searching for. A community of off-white figures clustered over the disintegrating pile. Granny's book is already in my hand, clutched tight as a talisman. I flick through the dog-eared pages to the right entry.

Faery Dreamer

The mushrooms are tiny, fragile things, shiny and sticky with a bell-shaped cap. They begin dark in spring but fade through the seasons. The paler the flesh, the more potent the mushroom. The gills are fine and dark and the spores black as pitch.

These fruitbodies are not for eating. Their mealy texture is not unpleasant, but

*the after effect often can be. They are not
known as Faery Dreamer for nothing.*

I shake out my cloth bag and kneel to
pick the mushrooms with gloved hands.
Dampness seeps from the ground and
through my skirts. The mushrooms are
small, delicate things, unassuming and
innocent. It would take the whole crop to
produce a jarful of powder. The last of
Granny's supply has dwindled to less
than a quarter of a jar. I harvest them all,
knowing fresh fruitbodies will sprout
again in a matter of days. That
mushrooms regenerate over and over,
from a fungus buried under the ground.
My bagful represents a tiny portion of the
whole and the larger part lives on.

I take the Faery Dreamers back to the
cottage and set them to dry. Then I leave
the gloves and bag beside the door to
wash separate from the rest of my
laundry. I take down the heavy book of
potions from the shelf and flick through
the pages.

Granny's graceful hand details the
method of creating the powder from the
mushrooms. The method of
administration. The various uses.

*Use sparingly as a strong pain-relief.
Resetting broken bones and suturing deep*

wounds. I do not recommend offering the Faery Dreamer to a woman in labour, as I have heard rumours of the baby arriving listless or developing slowly. There are, of course, situations where this is not a concern, and in these I advise you to provide as much relief for the woman as she requests. But when her labour is over and she lies empty armed, do not leave her side as she rides the dream, or allow her to sink, alone, into her grief.

I lift my puffy eyes from the page. As heavily as I rely on and as close as I may hold them, Granny's words are a poor substitute for her embrace and reassurance.

With a sigh, I set about packing a basket to take into the village. Cicely's husband has not called for me yet, but I include the last of Granny's powder just in case. Ready to help her through a labour that offers no hope at its end, when the time comes. To endure meaningless pain and strife, without reward.

I wade through the golden ocean of rye, whispering in the breeze. Whispering a secret that I must break to the farmer, yet dread speaking. Truth can be an agony; concealed truth an unbearable weight. I pick a head from the rye and compare it to the sketch in Granny's book one last time. Hoping that I am wrong but knowing I am not.

Purple Rooster's Spur

This fungus does not look like a mushroom. After a long, cold winter, an excessively wet spring may damage the young rye growing in the fields along the valley. Come harvest, you will find a long, hard, black protrusion growing from many of the grains. Warn the owners of the affected fields that his crop is diseased and must be burned. Eating the grains is the cause of Saint Anthony's Fire, a most terrible affliction.

I sigh and add the stalk to the bundle I have already collected. I brush through that diseased crop awaiting a harvest that will never be consumed. Towards the farmhouse, tiny on the hillside. I have a handful of silver in the purse on my belt to pay for the bunch in my hand. At least some good may come of this disaster, but the coins will be small recompense. My pace is slow with the thickness of the heat and reluctance to carry this burden of ill tidings.

When I get home, with a heavy heart and a lighter purse, I collapse onto the stool in my stone-walled kitchen and ease off my shoes. Granny's book of potions is laid out on the table, open at the entry I had been reading over breakfast. Purple Rooster's Spur. The first thing I thought of when I heard about the afflicted crop. The suspicion that I had just confirmed. The instructions on how to decoct a potion from the fungus.

This is a most beneficial substance to dry up the milk of a woman who suffers engorgement whilst weaning, or who never made use of the milk she produced. I add two drops to warm sage tea. The leaves of a savoy cabbage may also bring her some relief from the physical pain, but even time is a poor remedy for the emotional burden she bears.

It is cool in the cottage. The windows are small and the walls thick. I set about collecting the ingredients and apparatus Granny lists in the book, ready to create that potion for Cicely. And though I would never wish the destruction of a livelihood on anyone, I will not let the farmer's tragedy prevent me easing that of another. I carefully peel open the kernels of rye, exposing the black fungus growing inside.

The wheat fields beyond the paddock behind my cottage are loud with workers bringing in the harvest. The hillside is half stubble, where the scythes have been, and half rippling waves of gold. I pack myself a picnic lunch along with Granny's handbook, sling the basket over my shoulder and set off into the forest.

I follow the trail away from the village. The still air hums with tiny flies. I march through the clouds of them, sweat running down my spine. Birds sing, hidden in the shade. The hollow drumming of a woodpecker echoes through the trees. As I move further from humanity, my pace slows. I breathe deeper. Leaf mould and pine. A haze of yellow pollen drifts on a lazy breeze. I blow my nose on my handkerchief and wander on.

At mid morning, I pass the standing stones. I stop for a swig of water in the lee of the tallest one, back pressed against the cold smoothness. Then I set out again, deeper into the forest.

I reach the narrow gorge around midday and cross by the rickety bridge.

The ropes and wooden planks groan in complaint, but hold as I pass over the black emptiness below. The gentle trickle of water echoes from the rocky sides. The river is low but still running. Summer is near its end.

The path disappears into a bank of bracken. I struggle through, into the secret place Granny used to bring me. A hollow guarded by oak trees. A place that never feels warm, even on a day like today. I climb over the exposed roots and slide down the leaf strewn slope into the crater.

I sit on the old tree stump at the bottom and eat my lunch, leaving my crumbs for whichever beings dwell here. Fungi create steps around the stump at intervals just right for a tiny creature to ascend to my lap. I imagine them hopping up and down while I eat.

I don't need to check Granny's book, but I take it out anyway. I wonder if I will ever be able to identify a mushroom for myself without having her confirm my assessment for me. Were she still here she would laugh at me. But she isn't.

Lacquered Bracket Fungus

They form oyster-shaped ledges around hardwood tree stumps, as large as your *spread hand. The varnished surface is maroon, with concentric rings of purple, black, and red to show its seasons of growth and dormant anticipation. The stem is tough and snaps sharply when picked. When inverted, you can see the minute pores set in the brown skin. When sliced, the flesh inside is off-white with a rich, earthy fragrance.*

After lunch I leaf absently through the book. The well worn pages are still no substitute for Granny's company, but the absence has dulled over the past year. And then, when the sun slides behind one of the oaks, stealing what little warmth filtered down to me here, I collected a basketful of the Lacquered Bracket Fungus and scrambled back up the bank, beginning the long trek back into the world of other humans.

I reach the cottage not long before supper and cobble together a meal of salad and bread from the pantry. The basket lies on the table beside me. I retrieve the book from it and read as I eat.

The Lacquered Bracket Fungus is too tough to eat and tastes of soil and leaf mould and autumn. While the fungus is still fresh, dice it and submerge in good quality grain alcohol. Leave to steep for at least two moons, then drain through a cheese-cloth into a bottle. This tincture is a most efficient cure for low spirits if administered steadily over a period of several weeks. Any person in your care who seems to have lost their vitality and desire to connect with the living would benefit from a course of Lacquered Bracket Fungus tincture. But medication alone will not be enough. Ensure they are provided all the care and comfort and counsel they will accept. Ensure they do not become isolated. Watch their eyes for dark shadows and the skin of their wrists. Involve their family and neighbours. And listen silently when they open their lips.

I will prepare the tincture after supper. I hope I will not need it, that Cicely will rise naturally from her spiral of despair. But it is best to be prepared whilst continuing to hope. I push aside my empty plate and set to work.

I pull my hood over my head in an attempt to keep the drizzle off my face. At least the wind is coming from behind me. Brown leaves ride the gusts. I pull my cloak tighter around myself against the cold.

The track leading into the village grows progressively harder to travel as lanes branch out towards farms. By the time I reach the village, it's almost impassable. The churned mud at the edge looks promising. Yes – there against the steep side of the lane are growing the mushrooms I came hunting for. Dark and ragged in the mud. I open Granny's book under the cover of my cloak.

Grandfather Ink-Cap

The young fruitbody is white and egg-shaped and softly frilled. They grow in troops of four to eight, gaining height and losing girth through the season. These young specimens are an excellent addition to stews. But when the Grandfather Ink-Cap has reached the full length of your hand and the cap has opened into a scaly canopy with a tatty grey beard, they are ready to make ink.

I pick a dozen, which is more than enough for a bottle, and tuck them in beside the tincture in the bottom of my basket. I quicken my pace now that I'm not looking for the ink-caps. Hopefully I can reach Cicely's house before the rain gets any heavier.

Once I've made all of my visits and done all of my chores, I head home. The rain has set in, driving into my face. The wind tugs the hood off my head and drags the cloak out behind me so that it is no protection at all against the elements. When I burst through the kitchen door at last, I peel off every item of clothing, stoke the stove and drape them over it. Then I wrap myself in layer upon layer of blankets and sit on my stool at the table, poring through Granny's potion book.

Set the Grandfather Ink-Caps in a bowl at home and allow the black gills to deliquesce, filling the air around with dark spores. After a couple of weeks the Ink-Caps will have dissolved, leaving only a stem and a leathery skin from the cap. Strain the liquid into a bottle and stopper.

The ink keeps well, but does accumulate an unsavoury odour of rot after a week. This can be mitigated by adding a few drops of plant oil. I like the scent of rosemary myself, but others work just as well. The ink is smooth and uniformly black, bar the twinkle of spores left in the wake of your pen stroke.

I was taught as a child that the ink of the Grandfather Ink-Cap had the ability to transcend realms. That words written here on earth could be read by beings Elsewhere. If anyone comes to you with a request for help that you know is beyond the power of us mortals to give, have them peel the bark of a silver birch, and upon it write their request using a raven-feather quill and Grandfather Ink-Cap ink. Then send the petition away upon whichever is their native element.

The ink-caps lie in the basin on my kitchen windowsill for ten days, slowly converting to a thin black liquid. Then I bottle the ink, add lavender oil with a flush of boldness, and set out towards the village as I do every day, to check on Cicely.

The day is cold but dry. We walk together to the ridge at the top of the valley, wind nipping at our faces. On the way I collect a raven feather and birch bark. Nature provides for us once more. At the top of the ridge, I cut a crude nib into the feather. Cicely and I write our wishes onto our scraps of bark and then roll them tightly, hiding the words. Then I watch Cicely shred hers into strands and release them into the sky on the windy hilltop. I dig a hole into the sodden ground with my fingers and bury mine. The words we wrote travel away, on the wind and into the soil. Should anyone receive our requests, we can only hope that they have the power and compassion to answer them.

My nails are black with mud and I feel foolish. But then Cicely grins at me and we are foolish together. That is all the reward I could ever have hoped for. A wish too great to inscribe on birch bark. A magic that comes from within, not above, manifesting at the fringes of our shared humanity. The evidence of something deep and hidden. I smile back at her and we return to the village together.

I walk her back to her cottage, where her husband is fixing a trellis sagging off the side of their porch. We exchange pleasantries and I promise to call in on Cecily again tomorrow. Then I take the muddy track home.

On my way I stray into the woods. The air is rich with the fragrance of decomposition. Of the old preparing for the new. I wear the solitude like a garment that I can shrug off. No one item is designed for all seasons. The trick is finding the one that suits your present need.

The ground is damp and tangled with grasping understory, but I brush through boldly. I make my way towards a clump of Breast Feather fungus adorning a hazel trunk up ahead. I will make sure I have enough to make Cicely more tea, should she call round for it one day. And I will sit her down on the stool while I take the rocking chair, and I will teach her about mushrooms as she drinks.

See Hannah Hulbert's story "A Witch's Guide to Mushrooms and Toadstools" online at Metaphorosis.
If you liked it, leave a comment. Authors love that!
Remember to subscribe to our e-mail updates so you'll know when new stories are posted.

About the story

'A Witch's Guide to Mushrooms and Toadstools' is probably the only story I have ever written for which I can tell you exactly where and when it originated. My family and I were on a walk on 19th October at Avon Heath, not far from where we live. It was a bright, mild day and I took 36 photos of fungi. While the kids played in the stream, I read 'Sunday is Pancake Day' by Tyler Omichinski in *Aether and Ichor* (September 25 2019). The two elements combined to form Granny's field notes. Morris coached me through expanding these into a story — it would not exist without him, so he has my eternal thanks!

A question for the author

Q: If you could have any super power, what would it be?

A: One ability I always fancied was the Fool's skill-tipped fingers from Robin Hobb's 'Realm of the Elderlings'. The ability to know something intimately and completely by touching it. To know its past and future, its properties and potential. And the fact that such an ability can be turned off by simply wearing a glove. A low-key power with few responsibilities attached and hardly any chance of me becoming the target of a maniacal villain.

About the author

Hannah Hulbert lives in urban Dorset, UK. She is on a permanent sabbatical from reality as she raises two children and devotes her scarce free time to visiting imaginary worlds, some of her own creation. She has a degree in Ancient and Medieval History and an obsession with man-made places in the process of being reclaimed by nature. She is probably tweeting or doodling at this very moment.

@hhulbert

Exhibit 57-B
from the Trial of Alonzo Montalvo
v. MoodFoods Incorporated

Douglas DiCicco

Exhibit 57-B in the matter of Alonzo
Montalvo v. MoodFoods Incorporated is
brought to you by NeutralBot, today's
leading provider of AI-directed viewpoint-
neutral video analysis. NeutralBot:
because no humans means no bias.

This transcript has been enhanced
with NeutralNotes™, providing useful
context and analysis where deemed
appropriate by the NeutralBot AI. These
NeutralNotes™ have been crafted by our
state of the art AI to be relevant to Alonzo
Montalvo's claim that MoodFoods

Incorporated must indemnify him against any claims of assault, bodily injury, and/or property damage made by Maria Yevez, Steven Prosser, SceneBeyond Studios, or any of their affiliates or associates.

TRANSCRIPT BEGINS

(The video opens with a view of a black and white clapper board. The board indicates this is the first take of a commercial advertisement.)

Director Maria Yevez (hereafter, MY): Action!

(The clapper board is removed. Alonzo Montalvo stands smiling in front of a television set made to resemble a kitchen. Various MoodFoods Incorporated products are arranged on counters and tables behind him.)

Alonzo Montalvo (Party A) (hereafter, AM): Hello there! I'm Alonzo Montalvo, Emmy-nominated star of television's Open Heartbreak Surgery.

(NeutralNote™: AM's Emmy nomination was for a local award during his brief period as a news reporter in New Mexico. The nomination preceded the filming of the transcribed commercial by seventeen years.)

AM: As a famous Hollywood actor, I know how important it is to keep control over my emotions. You know, we all have days when we need to feel one way, but for one reason or another we're feeling something completely different. Don't you wish you could just change your emotions with a snap of your fingers? Well, now you can! That's why I'm here to talk to you about MoodFoods.

(The camera tracks AM and zooms in slightly as he moves to a counter where a MoodFoods brand JoyJelly has been plated. The orange coloration is consistent with Cantaloupe Contentment flavor.)

AM: If you're one of millions of Americans like me who sometimes needs a little pick me up to shake off the blues, you're probably already familiar with JoyJelly. Not only does this delicious gelatin dessert taste great, it actually gives you a powerful feeling of peace and happiness.

(AM picks up a spoon and carves out a bite of JoyJelly.)

AM: JoyJelly is not an antidepressant. There are no side effects. No addiction. It's just like a little spark of happiness right in your brain, perfect for bringing you out of a slump or starting your day with a little extra spring in your step.

(NeutralNote™: The preceding statement by AM is not consistent with current FDA labeling and advertising regulations applying to emotion-altering foodstuffs in general and MoodFoods in particular.)

(Party B disputes the neutrality of the preceding NeutralNote™.)

(AM eats the bite of JoyJelly.)

AM: Mmm-mmm! That is refreshing. Not only does it taste great and freshen my breath, I'm already feeling a... a...

(AM trails off. His lips are smiling, but there is fear in his eyes. Something has gone wrong.)

(Party B disputes the neutrality of the preceding line of transcription.)

AM: I'm sorry, can we cut?

MY: What's wrong? That take was going great.

AM: I think I'm feeling it. I mean, the happy feeling.

MY: So? That's what this stuff does. You're supposed to get the happy feeling.

AM: I thought we were using duds. I mean, ones without the stuff in them.

MY: It's fine. It'll just make it easier to pretend to be happy.

AM: I'm an actor. I pretend to be happy every day. I don't want to take a bunch of drugs while I'm working.

MY: They aren't drugs. They're single use nano—

AM: Fine, whatever, not the point. Can't we get some fake ones in here?

MY: I'm sorry, no. The FDA doesn't let us do that anymore. They say it's a form of false advertising.

(NeutralNote™: MY's statement is not an accurate reflection of current FDA advertising regulations. Her statement may be a reaction to recent class action litigation against MoodFoods Incorporated.)

(Party B disputes the neutrality of the preceding NeutralNote™.)

AM: (EXPLETIVE DELETED). Is this even safe? I mean, I'm going to be eating these things all day. The script says I'm supposed to take a bite of everything at one point or another.

MY: It'll be fine. Medical and legal cleared everything. They're not drugs. Besides, a lot of MoodFoods counteract the effects of other MoodFoods. It'll probably all cancel out in the end.

AM: ... Fine. Okay. I'm a professional. I'll get this done.

MY: That's the spirit. Cut. Let's get ready for take two, people.

(The video cuts to the clapper board. It indicates this is the second take.)

MY: Action!

Action proceeds in a fashion similar to the first take. AM's speech remains on script. For the sake of brevity, AM's speech is omitted from this transcript up until after he takes the first bite of JoyJelly.

AM: Mmm-mmm! That is refreshing. Not only does it taste great and freshen my breath, I'm already feeling a sense of euphoric calm. With JoyJelly those everyday anxieties and concerns just melt away. It's a milder alternative to chemical mood alteration, with none of the weight gain or sexual dysfunction associated with drug-based treatments. Mmm-mmm!

(AM takes a second bite of the JoyJelly.)

(NeutralNote™: According to Exhibit 36-A, MoodFoods Infomercial Script, this second bite was not part of the script for the infomercial.)

(Party B disputes the neutrality of the preceding NeutralNote™.)

AM: Delicious! But we can't just feel happy all the time, can we? The human experience is so much richer than that. Unending happiness from a blob of gelatin will ultimately feel hollow and meaningless without—

MY: Stop!

(AM looks off-camera to MY. His smile is broader than ever, but his eyes show annoyance.)

AM: What's the problem?

(MY steps in front of the camera to speak with AM.)

(NeutralNote™: At this point in the video, MY does not appear to have any of the scrapes, bruises, or other superficial injuries documented in Exhibit 16-A through 16-D, medical records of Maria Yevez.)

MY: You're off script.

AM: I know. I was ad-libbing.

MY: The whole point of the product is that people can eat it and feel happy. MoodFoods doesn't want you calling the sense of euphoria their product provides "hollow and meaningless". They certainly don't want you referring to the product as a "blob of gelatin". That's not the message we're going for here.

AM: I was trying to transition to the SadSoup segment. You know, explain why they'd want to use a product that makes them depressed. I still don't understand why anyone buys that stuff.

MY: Just stick to the script, please. Cut!

(Video cuts to the clapper board. This is the third take.)

MY: Pick it up from "but we can't just feel happy all the time". Action!

AM: But we can't just feel happy all the time, can we? What if you need to put yourself in the right frame of mind for a funeral, a memorial service, or a day of remembrance for a major national or international tragedy? Well, MoodFoods has you covered there, too.

(AM moves to another counter. A serving of SadSoup has been poured into a bowl. The empty can sits nearby. The label and green coloration of the soup are consistent with Sorrowful Spinach flavor. The camera zooms in to capture a close up of the bowl of soup and the label on the can.)

AM: Introducing SadSoup, the perfect appetizer to put you in a somber and reflective mood.

(AM ingests a spoonful of SadSoup.)

AM: With a sharp bitterness reminiscent of dark chocolate, SadSoup is perfect for serving at those occasions when you want everyone to be joined by a communal feeling of sorrow. Mmm. You know, this reminds me of my dog Max. He died just last…

(AM is visibly tearing up.)

AM: I'm sorry, can we cut again?

MY: What is it now?

(The video continues recording despite AM's request to cut.)

(NeutralNote™: Anecdotal evidence suggests SceneBeyond Studios camera operators are trained not to cut until the director personally calls for it.)

AM: The teleprompter says Max, but that wasn't my dog's name. My dog was named Rex.

MY: (quietly, sarcastic) How creative. There's that Emmy-winning talent.

AM: What?

MY: We made Max up for the script. It's not supposed to be about your real dog.

AM: Well, why can't it be? I mean, does it matter whether it's a fake name or not? I want to talk about Rex. I miss him.

MY: … Fine. I guess it doesn't matter. You can change the name to Rex if you stick to the rest of the script.

AM: I hadn't seen him for years. Cynthia got him in the divorce. So when I heard she'd put him down, I—

MY: Mr. Montalvo, I'm sorry, but we have to keep shooting. We have three more commercials to film today.

AM: You're right. I'm sorry. I'm so sorry.

MY: Cut.

(Cut to the clapper board. This is the fourth take.)

MY: Pick it up from "Introducing SadSoup". Action!

(AM repeats the lines and action in accordance with the script, including ingesting another spoonful of SadSoup.)

AM: You know, this reminds me of my dog Rex. He died just last year. It can be sad to think of loved ones we've lost over the years, but there's also a certain catharsis that comes with exploring those losses. Don't bother with expensive therapists and grief counselors. With SadSoup you can express the full depths of your loss and move on as a fuller, more complete person. MoodFoods—

(A microphone boom descends into view.)

(NeutralNote™: Visual analysis has determined with 98.7% certainty that this is the same microphone boom introduced into evidence as Exhibit 6. The blood stains present on Exhibit 6 are not yet present on the boom at this point in the recording.)

MY: Boom in the shot. (EXPLETIVE DELETED) Steve.

Sound Crewmember Steven Prosser (hereafter, SP): Sorry!

(NeutralNote™: For additional context, see Exhibit 9-A through 9-V, medical records of Steven Prosser.)

MY: Sorry, Mr. Montalvo. You were doing great. Let's keep it going.

(AM is now visibly crying.)

AM: (quietly) I'll keep it going. I'm a professional.

MY: Great. Let's get makeup in here. Cut!

(Cut to the clapper board. Fifth take. There are no signs of AM's tears when he reappears.)

MY: Pick it up from "Introducing SadSoup". Action!

(AM follows the script, including ingesting a third spoonful of SadSoup. AM begins to deviate from the script with the lines referencing the deceased dog.)

AM: You know, this reminds me of my dog, Rex.

(AM begins to cry again.)

AM: I should have kept him. I thought Cynthia would take care of him.

(EXPLETIVE DELETED). I thought she would take care of me. But I didn't deserve her. I never deserved her. It was all my fault. All my—

MY: Okay, okay. Stop. You know what? Take four was fine. We don't really need the last line of the SadSoup segment. If MoodFoods really wants it, we can throw together a deepfake in post. It's not like we're breaking the bank on our effects budget here.

(NeutralNote™: Per current Screen Actor's Guild's recommendations, MY's proposal does not represent best practices for professional film development. The ability of current deepfakes to provide quality comparable to trained actors remains a subject of significant debate and disagreement.)

AM: Cynthia's right. I'm a hack. She said nobody cares about a local Emmy from forever ago.

MY: Let's take ten, everyone. Someone get Mr. Montalvo another JoyJelly, please. And get makeup back in here. Cut!

(AM looks as if he is trying to say something to MY before the video cuts, but is unable to do so. He is sobbing too hard to form words. He is clearly profoundly haunted by the failure of his marriage and his personal responsibility for that failure.)

(Party A disputes the neutrality and factual accuracy of the preceding line of the transcript.)

(Clapper board. Take six.)

MY: Okay, we're picking it up from "What about those days".

AM: I'm sorry, can we hold on a second?

(The clapper is removed. AM stands behind a counter with a plated RageWich framed in the middle of the shot. The bright red coloration of the sauce is consistent with Cayenne Calamity flavor.)

MY: What's the problem?

AM: I just don't understand the appeal of this one. I mean, I didn't understand SadSoup either, but this makes even less sense. Who buys a sandwich that makes them angry?

MY: Anger is a very productive emotion, Mr. Montalvo.

AM: Is that the angle? Productivity? I didn't really get that from the script.

MY: Sure, why not? I'm starting to feel pretty angry myself, and I'm pretty sure we'll have produced an infomercial by the end of this. Now please, just stick to the script.

AM: Okay, sorry. I'm ready.

MY: Good. Picking it up from "What about those days". Action!

AM: What about those days when you really need to stand up for yourself? Are you tired of getting pushed around by your co-workers? Have an annoying neighbor you wish you finally had the courage to tell off? Sick of being polite to aggressive telemarketers? MoodFoods has you covered. Introducing RageWich: a concentrated dose of delicious anger packed between two slices of buttery belligerence.

(AM picks up the RageWich and takes a bite.)

AM: Mmm, spicy! With RageWich—

(The microphone boom from Exhibit 6 descends into view. No visible blood stains.)

MY: Boom in the shot. (EXPLETIVE DELETED)

AM: (EXPLETIVE DELETED), Steve!

SP: Sorry, sorry!

AM: That was (EXPLETIVE DELETED) perfect, Steve. And you (MULTIPLE EXPLETIVES DELETED)—

MY: Cut!

(Clapper board. Take seven.)

AM: (close to the camera, near MY) How the hell has he not been fired?

MY: (quietly) Steve's the studio head's nephew. Nothing I can do about it. (louder) Places!

(AM returns to his place by the counter with the RageWich.)

MY: Picking it up from "what about those days". Action.

AM: What about those days when you really need to stand up for yourself? Are you tired of getting pushed around by your co-workers? Have an annoying neighbor you wish you finally had the courage to tell off? Do you feel like just storming over to your ex-wife's place and finally telling her what you think of her and her new little boy toy?

(AM picks up the RageWich and takes another bite.)

AM: Maybe you want some answers about how they could afford a trip to Maui when they said they didn't have enough money for Rex's surgery. Well, RageWich gives you the confidence you need to—"

MY: You're off script again, Mr. Montalvo.

AM: (EXPLETIVE DELETED). I was ad-libbing. Ad. Libbing. Have you never shot a commercial before? Never worked with an actual professional actor? I'm giving you gold up here, and you just want me to stick to this (EXPLETIVE DELETED) script written by whatever film school dropout you—

MY: I wrote the script, Mr. Montalvo.

AM: (EXPLETIVE DELETED) you.

MY: Cut.

(Clapper board. Take eight.)

MY: Picking it up from "mmm, spicy". Action.

(AM takes another bite of the RageWich.)

MY: Mr. Montalvo, I think we have enough shots of you eating the sandwich. It's fine. You can skip it.

(AM makes a fist, crushing the remaining RageWich in his hand.)

AM: Don't tell me how to (EXPLETIVE DELETED) act.

MY: Cut! Take fifteen, every—

(Clapper board. Take nine.)

MY: We're skipping ahead to the SootheSalad segment. I think you could use it, Mr. Montalvo. We'll finish up the RageWich segment later. Picking it up from—

AM: Wait. Hang on. I want to say something.

(The clapper is removed. AM looks more composed. The crumbled RageWich has been cleaned up.)

MY: What is it now, Mr. Montalvo?

AM: I get it now. I get it. The products. Why anyone would want to buy these things. I can do this.

MY: I'm very glad to hear it. Now, picking up from—

AM: I can sell these. Just let me try something. Roll for a little while, let me make my own pitch. It's going to be good, I promise.

MY: Mr. Montalvo, I'm sorry if you don't like the script, but it's already been approved by MoodFoods. If you could just —

AM: Please. Let me have one take. Just one. If you don't like it, or it doesn't work, I promise I'll stick to the script religiously for the rest of the shoot. No more ad-libs. I promise.

MY: ... One take. One take only, Mr. Montalvo.

AM: Thank you.

MY: Action.

(The camera zooms in on AM. He is composed. Focused. He knows exactly what he wants to say about MoodFoods products and services.)

(Party B disputes the neutrality of the preceding line of the transcript.)

AM: To be human is to struggle. To struggle against outside forces, yes. Disease, war, the random unhappy accidents of fate. But more than that, it is a struggle against ourselves, our emotions. Our emotions come from deep inside ourselves. We give birth to them, but we can never truly master them. We are paralyzed by useless regrets. We set out in pursuit of self-destructive folly, directed by pointless rage. We waste years of our short, precious lives swaddled in the comforting lies of false happiness. For millennia, humans have been mere flotsam swept along in the rapids of an emotional current outside of our control. No more. Today, we can be free. Today, with MoodFoods—

(The microphone boom from Exhibit 6 descends into view. No visible blood stains.)

MY: Boom in the shot.

SP: (EXPLETIVE DELETED). Sorry.

MY: (EXPLETIVE DELETED).

AM: (EXPLETIVE DELETED). I don't have to (EXPLETIVE DELETED) take this. I'm a (EXPLETIVE DELETED) Emmy winner.

SP: (quietly) Local Emmy winner.

AM: I (EXPLETIVE DELETED) heard that!

(AM's face contorts with fury. He leaps over the counter, knocking the SadSoup, JoyJelly, and SootheSalad onto the floor.)

MY: Mr. Montalvo!

SP: (EXPLETIVE DELETED).

(AM stomps towards SP, knocking over the camera. The lens fractures, heavily distorting the video from this point forward. The only clearly visible area is a portion of the craft services table.)

SP: I'm sorry! I'm sorry!

AM: Rex!

(The audio is replaced with a loud crashing sound, followed by silence. Audio analysis suggests with 89.4% certainty that this is the result of Exhibit 6 striking a hard object with considerable force, breaking in the process. Given an 88.6% likelihood that the hard object in question is the face and/or torso of Steven Prosser, this is likely the source of the injuries documented in Exhibit 9-A through 9-V.)

(Several people can be seen running past the camera in an apparent state of panic. The speed at which they are moving combined with the damage to the camera lens makes most impossible to identify, with the exception of AM, who stops at the craft services table to take an entire platter of RageWiches.)

(Video ends.)

(NeutralNote™: The video time stamp places the end as seconds before the beginning of Exhibit 58-A, video of Alonzo Montalvo's rampage through the SceneBeyond Studios parking structure and subsequent arrest by local law enforcement.)

(NeutralNote™: Thank you for using NeutralBot. This transcript has been enhanced with insightful AI-generated analysis.)

(Party A and Party B dispute the neutrality and factual accuracy of the preceding NeutralNote™.)

TRANSCRIPT ENDS

See Douglas DiCicco's story "Exhibit 57-B from the Trial of Alonzo Montalvo v. MoodFoods Incorporated" online at Metaphorosis.
If you liked it, leave a comment. Authors love that!
Remember to subscribe to our e-mail updates so you'll know when new stories are posted.

About the story

The format of Exhibit 57-B comes from my background as an attorney. I've read many transcripts of bizarre exchanges over the years. I find something uniquely comical about seeing something strange and unexpected in such a dry, formal format. As for the actual content of the story, I wrote it as a way of exploring my thoughts about our current culture about emotional health, and the societal idea that it is almost always good to feel happy. There's an appropriate and an inappropriate way to feel about almost everything, and people sometimes try to force themselves to feel the "right" way in a given situation, even if it comes naturally. The story is about what happens when you take that way of thinking to an extreme.

A question for the author

Q: Is there a specific environment you find most conducive to writing, and is it different for different kinds of scenes?

A: I do almost all of my writing in my home office. I've tried writing in book stores, coffee shops, and at writer meetups in the past, but I've found I'm less productive with other people around.

The physical location is the same no matter what I'm writing, but I do change what I'm listening to. When I need calm focus I either listen to the sounds of rain or just have complete silence. When I'm looking for a more energetic mood, I switch to music.

About the author

Douglas DiCicco is a writer of speculative fiction. He has worked as an attorney, a teacher, and a renaissance faire performer. He currently lives with his wife, son, and cat in Clovis, California.

Copyright

Metaphorosis Publishing

Metaphorosis offers beautifully written science fiction and fantasy. Our imprints include:

Metaphorosis Magazine
plant based press
Metaphorosis Books
Driftwyrd
Vestige

Help keep Metaphorosis running at
Patreon.com/metaphorosis

See more about some of our books on the following pages.

Metaphorosis Magazine

Metaphorosis
a magazine of speculative fiction

Metaphorosis is an online speculative fiction magazine dedicated to quality writing. We publish an original story every week, along with author bios, interviews, and notes on story origins. Come and see us online at magazine.Metaphorosis.com

Keep Metaphorosis running! Support us at
Patreon.com/metaphorosis

You can also find us at:
Twitter: @MetaphorosisMag,
@MetaphorosisRev, @Metaphorosis
Facebook:
www.facebook.com/metaphorosis

We publish monthly print and e-book issues, as well as yearly Best of and Complete anthologies.

Metaphorosis: Best of 2019

The best science fiction and fantasy stories from *Metaphorosis* magazine's fourth year.

Metaphorosis 2019

All the stories from *Metaphorosis* magazine's fourth year. Fifty-two great SFF stories.

Metaphorosis: Best of 2018

The best science fiction and fantasy stories from *Metaphorosis* magazine's third year.

Metaphorosis 2018

All the stories from *Metaphorosis* magazine's third year. Fifty-two great SFF stories.

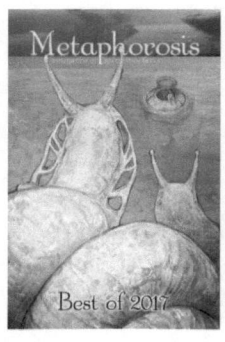 

Metaphorosis:
Best of 2017

The best science
fiction and fantasy
stories from
Metaphorosis
magazine's *second*
year.

Metaphorosis
2017

All the stories
from *Metaphorosis*
magazine's second
year. Fifty-three
great SFF stories.

Metaphorosis: Best of 2016

The best science fiction and fantasy stories from *Metaphorosis* magazine's first year.

Metaphorosis 2016

Almost all the stories from *Metaphorosis* magazine's first year.

Plant Based Press

plant
based
press

Vegan-friendly science fiction and fantasy, including an annual anthology of the year's best SFF stories.

Best Vegan SFF of 2019

The best vegan-friendly science fiction and fantasy stories of 2019!

Best Vegan SFF of 2018

The best vegan-friendly science fiction and fantasy stories of 2018!

Best Vegan SFF of 2017

The best vegan-friendly science fiction and fantasy stories of 2017!

Best Vegan SFF of 2016

The best vegan-friendly science fiction and fantasy stories of 2016!

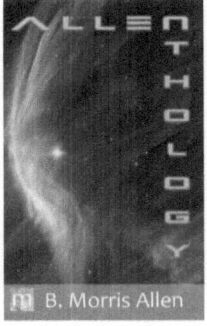

Susurrus

A darkly romantic story of magic, love, and suffering.

Allenthology: Volume I

A quarter century of SFF, including the full contents of the collections *Tocsin, Start with Stones,* and *Metaphorosis.*

Metaphorosis Books

Science fiction and fantasy books for writers – full of great stories, often with an additional focus on the craft of speculative fiction writing.

Score

an SFF symphony

What if stories were written like music? *Score* is an anthology of varied stories arranged to follow an emotional score from the heights of joy to the depths of despair – but always with a little hope shining through.

Reading 5X5

Five stories, five times

Twenty-five SFF authors, five base stories, five versions of each – see how different writers take on the same material, with stories in contemporary and high fantasy, soft and hard SF, and a mysterious 'other' category.

Reading 5X5

Writers' Edition

All the stories from the regular, readers' edition, plus two extra stories, the story seed, and authors' notes on writing. Over 100 pages of additional material specifically aimed at writers.